BUG BUDDIES

Slime
Time

With special thanks to Mariam Vossough

In memory of Matthew Eggleton, a true buddy

First published in paperback in Great Britain by
HarperCollins *Children's Books* in 2009
HarperCollins *Children's Books* is a division of HarperCollins *Publishers* Ltd,
77-85 Fulham Palace Road, Hammersmith, London W6 8JB.

Visit our website at: www.harpercollins.co.uk

1 3 5 7 9 10 8 6 4 2

Text copyright © Working Partners 2009
Illustrations copyright © Duncan Smith 2009

ISBN-13: 978-0-00-732248-0

Printed and bound in England by Clays Ltd, St Ives plc

Mixed Sources
Product group from well-managed
forests and other controlled sources
www.fsc.org Cert no. SW-COC-1806
© 1996 Forest Stewardship Council

FSC is a non-profit international organisation established to promote the
responsible management of the world's forests. Products carrying the FSC
label are independently certified to assure consumers that they come
from forests that are managed to meet the social, economic and
ecological needs of present and future generations.

Find out more about HarperCollins and the environment at
www.harpercollins.co.uk/green

Slime Time

JOE MILLER

Illustrated by Duncan Smith

HarperCollins *Children's Books*

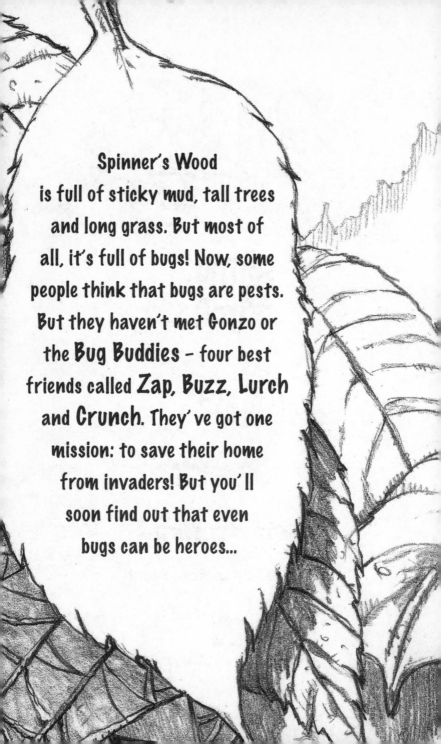

Spinner's Wood is full of sticky mud, tall trees and long grass. But most of all, it's full of bugs! Now, some people think that bugs are pests. But they haven't met Gonzo or the **Bug Buddies** – four best friends called **Zap**, **Buzz**, **Lurch** and **Crunch**. They've got one mission: to save their home from invaders! But you'll soon find out that even bugs can be heroes...

Contents

CHAPTER 1

Zap waved his wings to get Buzz's attention. He was standing unmarked, right by Centipede United's goal. If his friend passed him the apple-pip ball he could score!

Suddenly, a leaf blew on to the pitch in front of Buzz. The ladybird

dropped the ball and started
chomping on the juicy snack. Zap's
antenna sagged. They'd never win
now.

"What a time to stop for a nibble!"
said Lurch, darting in and grabbing the
apple pip.

"Over here!" shouted Zap.

Lurch hurled the seed in Zap's direction. The clover seed weevil flicked a wing and sent the ball flying straight into Centipede United's goal. Gonzo the grasshopper clicked to signal the end of the match.

"That's four-three to the Bug Buddies," shouted Gonzo.

"Yes!" cried Zap, soaring into the air, doing a loop-the-loop above the crowd.

When Zap landed back on the soft grass, Crunch the stag beetle tapped him on the back with one of his giant claws.

"Well done," he said.

Buzz and Lurch flew over to join them.

"Hurry up, everyone, it's time for the parade!" said Buzz.

Zap led the way as they flew over to Gonzo's Rock. The wise old grasshopper was already there, waiting for all the bugs of Spinner's Wood to gather.

Zap shivered as a dark shadow fell over them. He looked up to see thick, grey clouds forming in the sky. None of the other bugs seemed to notice, as they chattered excitedly.

Gonzo held up his front leg, signalling for the crowd to be silent. "Firstly, thank you for putting on such an exciting game," said the grasshopper. "What a great way to start our celebration day – **the day when we rename Spinner's Wood."**

Zap tingled with excitement. With Spinner, the nasty spider, banished forever, the bugs of the wood wanted no more reminders of his evil

existence. They were going to vote

on a new name for their home.

"OK, friends," said Gonzo. "Line up

for the victory parade."

Zap felt proud as he crawled to

his place.

"I can't believe I forgot to bring my dung ball," said Lurch.

"You say I'm mad about food," said Buzz. "You're even crazier about poo!"

"Oh!" cried Zap when a raindrop fell on his head.

More raindrops tumbled from the sky, followed by a loud rumble of thunder.

"I h-hate storms," said Crunch, hiding behind his claws.

Gonzo hopped back on to his rock.

"Everyone, take shelter," he said.

"The renaming ceremony is

postponed until tomorrow."

The sound of disappointed groans

filled the clearing.

"Let's go in there," cried Lurch, pointing towards a hole in an oak tree trunk. The Bug Buddies took shelter inside the tree hollow.

"It's a bit dark in here," said Crunch, nervously.

"At least we're safe and dry," said Zap. "It's raining really hard now!"

He peered outside. The leaves drooped and the branches rattled as raindrops thudded down. Zap shuddered. Suddenly, it felt eerily cold, as if trouble was waiting just around the corner...

CHAPTER 2

Zap opened his eyes and stretched his wings. Along with the rest of the Bug Buddies, he'd curled up in the tree trunk and had managed to sleep through the night, despite the rainstorm howling outside. Now the rain had cleared, but where were his friends?

He crawled out of the hollow to
see that the ground was covered in
sticky mud.

"About time, sleepyhead," cried a
familiar voice.

Zap looked round to see Crunch
and Buzz crawling towards him.

"Where's Lurch?" he asked.

"Here!" shouted Lurch, appearing
from behind a bush. He was pushing a
large dung ball, which kept getting
stuck in the thick mud.

"Perhaps we should rename it
Muddy Wood!" said Lurch, puffing.

"I'm so excited about today, I couldn't eat breakfast," said Buzz.

"Really?" said Zap, surprised.

"Well… I only had one serving instead of two," replied Buzz.

Zap laughed as he flew off. "Come on," he said. "Let's give this wood a new name!"

Zap, Buzz and Crunch flew towards Gonzo's Rock, with Lurch crawling along with his dung ball beneath them. A strange glistening kept on catching Zap's eye. He felt uneasy as

he looked about. *The wood seems
different somehow,* he thought, *but I
can't quite figure out why.*

Zap whizzed round a corner to fly
up Leafy Lane and stopped dead.

"Whoah!" said Crunch. "What's
wrong?"

"Take a look," said Zap, pointing his
antennae.

Leafy Lane, where the box elder
bugs lived, was usually full of lush
trees and shiny green and white hosta
plants. But now the trees were
stripped of their leaves and the plants

had been eaten back to their stalks.

"Giddy grasshoppers!" cried Buzz.

"Looks like the box elder bugs
were even hungrier than Buzz," said
Lurch.

A group of them crawled towards
the Bug Buddies. Their deep red eyes
looked sad.

"It wasn't us," said a small box elder. "It was like this when we woke up."

"We can't even eat what's left," said another, his tummy rumbling. "Every plant is covered in sticky slime."

Zap looked around. Trails of slime criss-crossed the lane, glistening in the sunlight. He'd seen that same glistening all over the wood this morning…

"We need to talk to Gonzo, right now!" he said.

The Bug Buddies arrived at Gonzo's Rock to find lots of bugs crowded around the grasshopper.

"We're starving," said a green tiger beetle. "All our food is gone."

"And new plants can't grow through the thick slime on the ground," an earwig said.

Zap crawled forwards. "It's true. Nearly all the leaves have been eaten and there's slime everywhere."

"Suck sap out of the stalks," said Gonzo. "That will keep you going for now. We need to work out who's doing this before there's no food left anywhere."

The grasshopper looked down at Zap with his large, green eyes. *He wants* me *to figure this out,* Zap thought, his mind buzzing. *What creature is slimy?* Suddenly, an image formed in Zap's mind – a huge grey body and tentacles waving in the air. *That's it!* he thought.

"I met a nasty-looking slug at Stinking Bog," said Zap. "What if it's him?"

"That's certainly possible, good

27

thinking," said Gonzo, nodding approvingly.

"Oh, that sneaky slug!" said Buzz. "Perhaps he doesn't know the rules of Spinner's Wood yet," replied Gonzo, calmly. "Why don't you invite him here? I can explain that all the food needs to be shared equally. We'll have to postpone the renaming ceremony until afterwards,

though. This is urgent."

Zap zoomed up into the air,

flapping his wings with all his might.

"Come on, Bug Buddies!" he cried.

"Let's go to Stinking Bog!"

CHAPTER 3

Zap led the way through the wood.
The golden glow of the sun warmed
his body as they reached the edge of
Stinking Bog. Unfortunately, it had
also heated up this swampy part of
the wood.

"It pongs," moaned Buzz, wrinkling

his face up.

"It's a bit

whiffy, even for

me!" said Lurch.

Zap looked over

to where he'd first met the

slug. He was nowhere to be seen.

"Let's split up," he said. "The

sooner we find that slug, the better."

The Bug Buddies began searching.

Zap flew low to the ground,

exploring every leaf and bush, but the

area was slug-free. Suddenly, a beam

of sunlight burst through the trees.

It lit up a thick trail of slime on the
path below.

"Found something!" shouted Zap.

The others flew over to join him.
Zap took the lead. The slime trail led
to a group of fat grey slugs in the
shade, chomping on mushrooms
on the far side of the bog, their
bellies swelling with every bite.

"Don't they *ever* stop eating?" whispered Lurch.

"Hello," called Zap, walking forwards to greet them.

A couple of slugs raised up their eyestalk tentacles to look at him. The largest one blew a spit bubble at Zap, and another one did a loud belch.

"How rude!" said Buzz.

"Where is your leader?" Zap
asked. "I need to invite him to a
meeting at Gonzo's Rock."

The slugs finally stopped eating.
With the largest slug at the front,
they crawled slowly towards him.

Zap shivered as their thick,
muscular bodies squelched along the
ground, leaving a trail of slime behind
them.

"You were right," whispered Buzz.
"That's the same slime that we saw in
Leafy Lane."

The Bug Buddies huddled close as the slugs formed a circle around them.

"What are they doing?" asked Crunch.

"I'm not sure," said Zap, worried.

But I must get them to listen, he thought, *otherwise there will be no food left in the whole wood!!*

The largest slug slithered forwards, his eyes fixed on Zap.

"Don't you know anything about slugs?" he said. "Our leader won't go to Gonzo's Rock in this sunshine."

"But it's important," said Zap.

"Why?" asked the slug. "What does Gonzo want with the Slime King?"

The Bug Buddies looked at each other and laughed. It was the funniest thing Zap had ever heard.

"Slime King!" said Buzz, chuckling. "What a silly name!"

The Bug Buddies hugged their bellies as they collapsed into giggles. The slug's face creased with anger. He nodded to the other slugs, and they began to close in on the Bug Buddies.

"Oh dear," whispered Zap. "I don't think it was a good idea to laugh at their king."

"Sorry guys," said Buzz, quickly. "We were only joking."

Zap gulped as the slugs got even closer. It looked like they were going to attack…

"You won't be laughing when we've

finished with you," said the largest
slug.

Zap launched himself into the air,
soaring high above the slugs and
shouting to his friends, **"Get in the
air, quick!"**

CHAPTER 4

Back on Gonzo's Rock, the grasshopper listened thoughtfully as the Bug Buddies told him what had happened.

"Those horrid bullies said their Slime King won't come out in the sun," said Zap.

"That's because slugs shrivel up in the heat," explained Gonzo.

"But how are we going to stop him destroying the wood if he only comes out in the rain?" asked Zap. "That's when every other bug takes cover!"

"Maybe that's not the *only* time slugs come out," replied Gonzo. "Work out when else they appear and you might be able to stop him."

Zap looked up at Gonzo, hoping he would tell them some more. But the

wise old grasshopper stayed quiet. *He wants us to solve this one by ourselves,* thought Zap.

"Good luck," said Gonzo. "I have to do my rounds and check how much food is left."

Zap watched him hop away, disappearing amongst the long grass.

"What if we can't work out where else to find the slugs?" said Lurch, worried.

"We must," replied Zap. "The future of the wood depends on us."

The Bug Buddies flew over to Algae Pond to think things over. As he sipped at the water, deep in thought, Zap felt a gentle tug on his wing. He looked round to see some baby grasshoppers staring at him with a sad look in their tiny green eyes.

"Our bellies are grumbling," said the littlest one.

Zap flew over the pond and fished out a leaf to give to the hungry grasshoppers.

"Here," he said. "This should fill you up."

"Thanks, Zap," said the grasshopper. "You're the best!"

The babies hopped off to eat the

leaf. Zap's own belly started to moan.

A large cloud moved across the sun, casting the whole of Algae Pond in shadow.

"I hate it when the clouds do that," said Crunch. "It makes it feel like night." **"I've got it!"** Zap cried.

"The slugs attacked during the rain when we were asleep. *That's* when the slugs come out – night time!"

Lurch flapped his wings excitedly. "Brilliant!"

"I'll stay up tonight and wait to see if they have another midnight feast," said Zap. "Who's with me?"

"Count me in!" said Buzz.

"Me too," said Lurch.

Crunch raised a claw nervously into the air. "And me," he said. "Even though I'm afraid of the dark."

The Bug Buddies were a strong team. But the thought of meeting the Slime King in the dark, shadowy wood sent shivers down Zap's wings…

CHAPTER 5

That night, the Bug Buddies made
their way over to Stinking Bog. A
group of friendly fireflies had joined
them to light the way. Their bodies
gave off a warm, yellow glow that
made it easier to forget about what
might be lurking in the darkness.

They arrived at the far side of the bog where the slugs had been. Now, there was no sign of movement.

"Maybe they're still asleep," whispered Crunch.

'Let's take a closer look," said Zap.

"Sometimes I wish our bodies didn't light up," said a firefly, nervously. "I don't want the slugs to spot us."

"Well, I'm glad that they do," replied Zap, smiling. "*And* I'm glad you're all so brave."

The fireflies held their heads high

 **47**

and flew beside Zap, lighting up the slugs' lair. Zap's wings drooped as he saw fresh trails of slime leading away from the bog.

"We're too late!" cried Lurch. "The slugs are already on the move."

"The Bug Buddies are *never* too late," said Zap. **"Follow that slime!"**

Zap zoomed out of the bog, flying so fast he overtook the fireflies and had to squint to see in the gloom. He swerved to avoid tall trees looming up out of the darkness. Zap was relieved about one thing – now that

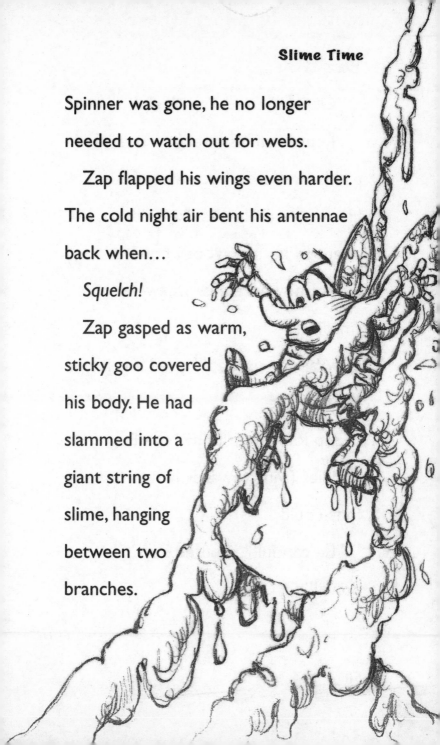

Spinner was gone, he no longer

needed to watch out for webs.

Zap flapped his wings even harder.

The cold night air bent his antennae

back when...

Squelch!

Zap gasped as warm,

sticky goo covered

his body. He had

slammed into a

giant string of

slime, hanging

between two

branches.

"Oh no!" cried Zap. "Help!"

He used all his strength to try and pull himself free, but it was no use. He was stuck. It was like being wrapped in thick, gooey honey — except nowhere near as sweet-smelling.

"Wait for us, Zap!" cried a voice in the distance.

Zap looked up to see the Bug Buddies flying towards him as fast as they could.

"Be careful!" shouted Zap. "Slow down!"

Buzz's eyes widened as he saw the net of slime.

"Whooo-aaah," he shouted, swerving to avoid it.

Lurch, Crunch and the fireflies also managed to dodge out of the way. Zap's friends hovered beside him.

"Don't worry, Zap," said Crunch. "I'll soon have you out of there."

The stag beetle used his large claws to hack away at the slime.

There was a slurping noise as Zap pulled himself free. He shook his body clean, but specks of goo still

clung on to his wings.

"You should wash that off," said Buzz.

"Not now, we've got slugs to catch," said Zap. "But this time, I'll watch where I'm flying."

Zap flew slowly. The sticky slime on his wings made it hard to flap them. With the fireflies to light the way, he followed the slime trail further into the wood. It led towards Algae Pond, where the sound of loud **BURPING** filled the air.

"I think we've found them," said Zap.

The Bug Buddies flew forwards and
peeped out from behind a bush.
There were loads of slugs, chewing
their way through the plants around
the pond.

"Once we've eaten all thisss," said a slithery voice, "we'll go and ssscoff whatever isss left at SSShadow Creek."

I know who that voice belongs to, thought Zap.

He turned to the fireflies. "Shine your brightest light on those slugs," he whispered.

The fireflies darted above the slugs. Their yellow glow lit up the whole group. All of the slugs immediately stopped eating.

"Why are you ssshining that light

on usss?" shouted the slithery voice.

Zap flew forwards nervously, glad that the Bug Buddies were right beside him. He spotted the Slime King straight away. He was even bigger than he remembered. His large, squidgy body oozed thick slime.

"*I* told them to shine it on you,"
said Zap, his legs shaking with nerves.

The Slime King stared at the little
weevil, an evil glint in his eyes.

**"You dare disssturb a ssslug
king while he isss eating?"** he
said. "You must be very brave… or
very ssstupid."

CHAPTER 6

"He's huge," said Crunch. "He could squash a bug to death!"

The stag beetle wasn't the only one who was nervous. Zap felt his wings trembling. It was night time and the whole wood was asleep. Whether they liked it or not, they had to face this monster slug alone.

"Get lossst, bugs!" snarled the
Slime King. "Leave usss to our feassst."

Even though he was scared, Zap
knew they couldn't give up. Not while
all the other creatures in the wood
were going hungry. He took a deep
breath.

"You must stop eating *all* of the
food," he said. "You have to share with
the rest of the bugs in the wood."

The Slime King laughed, his body
rippling.

"SSSlugs don't ssshare," he said.

"No one's going be friends with you, if you don't," said Lurch.

"Our only friend isss...FOOD," said the Slime King.

"If you stop now, Gonzo will give you a second chance," said Zap. "He gave Spinner loads more than that."

The giant slug narrowed his eyes at Zap.

"I ssshould have lissstened to SSSpinner before he left," he hissed. "He told me what a pessst you were. No one keepsss me away from my dinner!"

Chomp! The Slime King took a huge bite out of a bog bean plant. **Munch! Chomp! Munch!** His slugs did the same, hungrily eating their way around the pond.

"What are we going to do?" asked Buzz.

"I don't know," said Zap. "But we've got to stop them!"

Lurch flapped excitedly. "Why don't we tempt them away from the plants by giving them something else to eat?" he said.

Zap watched, puzzled, as Lurch scuttled off behind an elm tree. He quickly returned pushing a dung ball.

"I spotted it on the way here," he said.

Lurch pushed the dung ball towards the nearest group of slugs.

"Here, sluggies," he said. "This is tasty!"

The slugs laughed at him. "Only dirty dung beetles eat poo," said one.

"Don't you call my friend dirty!" yelled Crunch.

Zap was amazed to see Crunch crawling towards the slugs, not looking scared at all. He lowered his antlers and tried to pick up a slug in

his claws. But the slippery

creature slid easily out of his grasp.

"Can't catch me," laughed the slug.

"They're too slimy for me to grab!"

said Crunch, disappointed.

"My turn now," said Buzz. "How about I rush around and eat everything before the slugs can get to it? Then they'll *have* to go somewhere else to look for food."

Buzz set off, chomping at the leaves. He only managed to eat one plant before he crawled back to them and slumped on to the ground.

"My belly hurts," he groaned.

Crunch rubbed the ladybird's tummy. "That's why you shouldn't eat too much," he said.

"You're right!" said Zap, his

antennae pricking up. "That's given me
an idea!"

Zap gathered his friends round in
a huddle. "Instead of trying to stop
the slugs eating," he said, "we should
let them keep on scoffing."

"But that's exactly what we don't
want to happen," said Lurch,
confused.

"Oh yes, we do," said Zap. "Trust
me!"

CHAPTER 7

The Bug Buddies waited and watched
as the slugs stuffed themselves full of
food.

Buzz groaned and rubbed his
tummy. "Watching them eat makes
my belly feel even worse."

"We should help speed things up,"

said Zap, flying over to a bog bean

plant and pulling off a large leaf. He

dragged it across to the Slime King.

"Sorry for being so bossy earlier,"

said Zap.

The Slime King eyed the leaf,

suspiciously. Another slug slid up

beside him, his mouth open, ready to

eat it. The Slime King barged the

other slug out of the way.

"Mine!" he snapped, quickly

taking a big bite.

I knew he couldn't resist, thought

Zap.

Buzz, Crunch and Lurch helped Zap collect more treats for the slugs. The fireflies followed them, lighting the way. They'd soon gathered a massive pile of food, which the slugs greedily demolished.

"Thisss isss ssslug heaven," cried the Slime King, sap dripping down his face.

"And I thought Buzz ate a lot," said Lurch.

"Don't they *ever* get full?" said Crunch.

A tingle of nerves flitted through Zap's body. *Oh no,* he thought. *What if the slugs never get full? What if they eat and eat and eat until there's nothing left?*

Buzz pointed to the far side of the pond. "Seems like they do, Crunch."

Zap looked round to see that the slimy creatures had become so bloated, they couldn't move.

"The plan's working," he cried.
"Time for action!"

Zap and the fireflies flew across
the water and landed next to an
overfed slug. Zap and Crunch leaned
their front legs against the creature,
pushing him towards a muddy slope
away from the water. It was hard
work, but the slug was too full up to
fight back. The Bug Buddies paused
when they reached the top of the
slope. At the bottom was a path
leading out of the wood.

"This is *your* path – far away from

our food!" said Zap, giving the slug

one final shove.

"Ahhhh!" shouted the slug as he

rolled down the wet mud and out of

sight.

One at a time, the Bug Buddies
pushed the groaning slugs away down
the muddy slope. Finally, there was
only one slug left... **one very big
slug.**

Zap looked at the Slime King, who
was still blissfully unaware, tucking
into the pile of food.

"Come on Bug Buddies, let's finish
this!" he said.

The Bug Buddies crawled over to the giant slug. They stood in a line along his body and pushed as hard as they could. The slug looked stunned as he began to roll over.

"Hey! Ssstop!" he shouted. "I haven't finissshed eating."

"Oh yes, you have," said Zap.

The Slime King whipped his tentacles at Zap, trying to flick him aside.

"Quickly," said Zap. "We need to push harder!"

The Slime King tried his best to

slide away, but his belly was too bloated for him to move. "It's againssst ssslug law to leave food uneaten!" he protested.

Zap and friends finally rolled him to the top edge of the muddy slope.

"After three," said Zap. **"One, two, three!"**

The Bug Buddies shoved with all their might. Zap smiled as the Slime King rolled down the slope.

"Bye, bye greedy guts," shouted Lurch.

"I'll… be… back," said a slithery voice from the darkness.

Not if I've got anything to do with it, thought Zap.

CHAPTER 8

The soft light of dawn began to creep over Spinner's Wood. The Bug Buddies made their way back to Gonzo's Rock, where they told the grasshopper how they had defeated the slimy creatures.

"So, you made sure that the slugs'

own greed was their downfall," said Gonzo, nodding. "Very clever, Zap."

"It was Buzz who gave me the idea," said Zap.

"You four are quite a team," said Gonzo.

"Bug Buddies are the best!" said Lurch.

"I've got one final job for you," said the grasshopper. "Gather everyone together. It's about time we renamed this wood!"

The sun was high in the sky by the

time all of the bugs had made their
way to the clearing. Gonzo stood on
the rock, looking down at the crowd
and the Bug Buddies.

"I can't see one bug who isn't
smiling," said Zap, happily.

The air buzzed with excitement as
Gonzo clicked for silence.

"Yet again, we must thank our four
brave young friends," said Gonzo.
"Because of them, it won't be long
before new leaves grow and soon
there will be plenty of food for
everyone."

"Hooray for the Bug Buddies,"

shouted a group of butterflies.

Zap shuffled his feet, embarrassed,

as the crowd cheered.

"Now, it's time to make a choice,"

said Gonzo, quietening them down. "What will it be – Sunshine Wood or Chestnut Wood?"

But before any bug had the chance to vote, Zap spoke up.

"I have a better idea," he shouted. "Why don't we rename it Gonzo's Wood? After all, it's you who has kept us safe all these years."

Now it was Gonzo's turn to look embarrassed. He lowered his head as the crowd of bugs let out a mighty cheer.

"Gonzo! Gonzo!" they cried.

"Well?" said Zap, turning to his grasshopper friend.

"Looks like the bugs have spoken," Gonzo said, smiling.

Zap turned to his friends, a huge grin spreading across his face.

"Welcome to Gonzo's Wood!" he cried.

GREAT GREY
SLUGS

NAME: The Slime King

FAMILY: Limacidae

SIZE: Up to 20cm

DISLIKES: Slippery mud slopes, being told to stop eating, dry places, salt.

FUN FACTS: Unlike snails, slugs don't have a large protective shell to hide in, meaning that they are in more danger of drying out – and of being eaten!

Producing slimy mucus helps to keep slugs from drying out, as well as helping them slide along the ground. They can also produce stickier mucus which stops them from sliding down steep surfaces, but it's not much use on slippery mud slopes!

Most slugs have two sets of tentacles (or 'feelers') on their heads. The top pair lets them see, and the bottom pair lets them smell!

Have you read all these bug-tastic books?

BUG BUDDIES

The Big Game

It's the Beetle Ball final and the Bug Buddies face the mighty Centipede United. But who's lurking on the sidelines? Could it be Spinner?

OUT NOW!

BUG BUDDIES

Enemy Attack!

Spinner's Wood is under attack! The Bug Buddies think a certain spider is up to his old tricks. But is a new enemy on the prowl?

OUT NOW!

BUG BUDDIES

Ant Invasion!

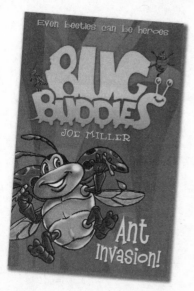

It's party time and the yellow ants are happy to share their yummy food with the Bug Buddies. But is there something funny in the honey? What could the ants be up to...

OUT NOW!

BUG BUDDIES

Tunnel Trouble

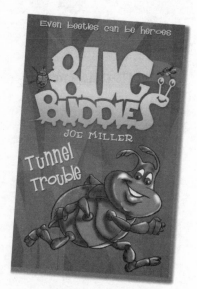

A storm is coming and scary tiger beetles need shelter. But can the Bug Buddies trust them? And is Spinner really gone for good?

OUT NOW!

BUG BUDDIES

Beetle Power!

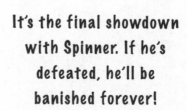

It's the final showdown
with Spinner. If he's
defeated, he'll be
banished forever!

OUT NOW!

JOE MILLER

Buy more great Bug Buddies books direct from
HarperCollins *Publishers*: at 10% off recommended
retail price. FREE postage and packing in the UK.

The Big Game	**ISBN: 978-0-00-731039-5**
Enemy Attack!	**ISBN: 978-0-00-731040-1**
Ant Invasion!	**ISBN: 978-0-00-731041-8**
Tunnel Trouble	**ISBN: 978-0-00-731042-5**
Beetle Power!	**ISBN: 978-0-00-732247-3**
Slime Time	**ISBN: 978-0-00-732248-0**

All priced at £3.99 RRP

More books coming soon!

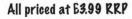